Kofi Kingston
NICE GUYS FINISH FIRST

by Tracey West

GROSSET & DUNLAP
An Imprint of Penguin Group (USA) Inc.

GROSSET & DUNLAP
Published by the Penguin Group
Penguin Group (USA) Inc., 375 Hudson Street, New York, New York 10014, USA
Penguin Group (Canada), 90 Eglinton Avenue East, Suite 700,
Toronto, Ontario M4P 2Y3, Canada
(a division of Pearson Penguin Canada Inc.)
Penguin Books Ltd., 80 Strand, London WC2R 0RL, England
Penguin Group Ireland, 25 St. Stephen's Green, Dublin 2, Ireland
(a division of Penguin Books Ltd.)
Penguin Group (Australia), 250 Camberwell Road, Camberwell, Victoria 3124, Australia
(a division of Pearson Australia Group Pty. Ltd.)
Penguin Books India Pvt. Ltd., 11 Community Centre, Panchsheel Park,
New Delhi—110 017, India
Penguin Group (NZ), 67 Apollo Drive, Rosedale, Auckland 0632, New Zealand
(a division of Pearson New Zealand Ltd.)
Penguin Books (South Africa) (Pty.) Ltd., 24 Sturdee Avenue,
Rosebank, Johannesburg 2196, South Africa

Penguin Books Ltd., Registered Offices: 80 Strand, London WC2R 0RL, England

ISBN 978-0-448-45906-6   10 9 8 7 6 5 4 3 2 1

Who says you have to break the rules to become a WWE Superstar? Kofi Kingston is one Superstar who has always played fair in and out of the ring. The athlete they call the Dreadlock Dynamo proves that you don't have to be a bad guy to succeed.

Kofi joined the WWE as a Superstar on ECW. Before he entered the ring, cameras caught Kofi helping out some kids on a beach. When a jerk knocked over their sand castle, Kofi tossed the rude dude into the ocean.

In his first televised match, Kofi ran into the ring with tons of energy. When his opponent, David Owen, clotheslined him, he popped right back up with a big smile on his face. He easily won the match, pinning Owen after knocking him down with a jump kick.

"A very impressive debut for Kofi Kingston!" the announcer cheered.

Soon Kofi was taking on the big guys. He faced former Intercontinental Champion Shelton Benjamin in an Extreme Rules match. Benjamin slammed Kofi into steel steps and pummeled him with garbage cans and a folding chair.

But Kofi rallied, battering Benjamin with a garbage can lid and then finishing him off with his now-famous jump kick: Trouble in Paradise.

Right after that match, Kofi was drafted to *Raw* and quickly got a shot at the Intercontinental Championship. At the 2008 Night of Champions, he faced Chris Jericho.

A champion many times over, Jericho was about to pin Kofi when Shawn Michaels climbed into the ring. Jericho went after Michaels, and Kofi jumped up and used Trouble in Paradise to take down Jericho. Kofi took home his very first WWE championship that night.

Kofi continued to prove that he wasn't just a champion—he was a good guy. At Unforgiven in 2008, CM Punk was being interviewed backstage when Randy Orton interrupted him. Then Cody Rhodes, Ted DiBiase, and Manu attacked CM Punk.

Kofi Kingston came to Punk's rescue. He rushed to the scene and tried to throw the three Superstars off of Punk. After all, three against one is never fair!

After that, Kofi and Punk teamed up. They took on World Tag Team Champions Cody Rhodes and Ted DiBiase on *Raw*. Rhodes and DiBiase used a lot of illegal moves. But no matter what they did, they couldn't take down Kofi and Punk.

Punk slammed DiBiase into the corner. Even though he wasn't tagged, Rhodes ran out. Kofi jumped into the ring and sent Rhodes tumbling over the ropes. That left his partner free to slam DiBiase with a GTS and pin him. Kofi and Punk were the new World Tag Team Champions!

Before the year was over, Kofi and Punk would lose the championship to John Morrison and The Miz. This began a rivalry between Kofi and The Miz, a conceited Superstar with a big mouth.

In a later interview, when Kofi was asked to name the most annoying Superstar, he had one clear answer: The Miz.

But Kofi didn't let the loss get him down. He went on to aim for bigger championships—and bigger Superstars. A month later, he took on seven-foot-tall giant Kane.

Kane pummeled Kofi at the start of the match, but then Kofi surprised the Big Red Monster with a jump kick to the chin. Angry, Kane lifted Kofi over his shoulder and went to drop him, but Kofi brought Kane with him on the way down. Once they were on the mat, Kofi quickly pinned

In the summer of 2009, Kofi got his chance to win the United States Championship. His opponent, MVP, was a Superstar he really respected. The two fought a clean match, a true test of skills. In the end, Kofi became the new United States Champion!

Over the next four months, Kofi defended the title nine times. Then his old rival, The Miz, wanted a shot. The two faced off in a high-energy match on *Raw*. Kofi dominated for most of the match, using all his best moves.

But then The Miz got lucky. Kofi tried to slam him into a corner, and The Miz slipped out. Kofi crashed into the corner instead. The Miz grabbed the dazed Kofi and delivered his Skull-Crushing Finale, slamming him headfirst into the mat. Kofi lost his championship when The Miz pinned him.

A few weeks later at Bragging Rights, Kofi reminded everyone that he was still a nice guy. At the event, Randy Orton battled John Cena in a championship. Orton's friends Cody Rhodes and Ted DiBiase ran into the ring and attacked Cena.

Kofi to the rescue! With the help of a folding chair, he chased the two Superstars backstage, and Cena became the new WWE Champion. Kofi did the right thing— but it led to a bitter rivalry with Orton.

Randy Orton, The Viper, got back at Kofi quickly. After Kofi faced Chris Jericho on *Raw*, Orton attacked him by surprise, throwing him to the floor.

Even nice guys get mad sometimes. Later that night, when Orton was in the ring, Kofi appeared on the TitanTron screen. While Orton watched, Kofi trashed Orton's brand-new race car. He poured orange paint over the image of Orton on the car's hood.

"Randy, if you ask me, I don't think you've ever looked better!" Kofi cried.

Two weeks later on *Raw*, Orton attacked Hall of Famer "Rowdy" Roddy Piper. Kofi came to the rescue again, and he and Orton began a brutal brawl.

The hard-core unofficial match ended when Kofi tossed Orton into the announcer's pit. He picked him up and placed Orton on a table. Then Kofi climbed on top of the railing and landed a Boom Drop on Orton, breaking the table in half.

"I don't think anybody realized Kofi had this in him," the announcer said.

The rivalry between the Superstars got fierce. At Survivor Series, Kofi and Orton each led a team in an elimination match. One by one, each Superstar that got pinned left the match. In the end, it was Kofi against Orton and his old partner, CM Punk.

It looked like there was no way Kofi could win. But he surprised everyone. Orton stayed outside the ring while Kofi battled Punk. When Kofi slammed Punk into the ring, Orton jumped in. Punk tried to pin a distracted Kofi, but Kofi turned the tables on him. After he pinned Punk, he hit Orton with a Trouble in Paradise. Orton was out, and Team Kofi was victorious.

The viper struck back last. A week later, Kofi and Orton had a match on *Raw*. Before the match even started, Orton had Cody Rhodes and Ted DiBiase attack Kofi backstage. Kofi insisted on facing Orton even though he was hurt. In the end, Orton pinned Kofi—and kept on pummeling him even after the bell rang.

But the rivalry between the two Superstars still wasn't over.

On the last *Raw* of 2009, Kofi had a chance to earn the United States Championship. If he beat the current United States Champion, The Miz, in a non-title match, he could have a title match that same night.

The first match was a short one. The Miz climbed the ropes, but when he jumped down, Kofi nailed him with a Trouble in Paradise. The Miz was knocked out, and Kofi pinned him easily.

The second match began immediately. Kofi dominated a still-dazed Miz. He knocked him down with a leg sweep and then slammed him with a Boom Boom Drop. He topped it off with a Trouble in Paradise, and victory was just three counts away.

Out of nowhere, Orton ran up and pulled Kofi out of the ring. He rammed Kofi's head into the steel ring post and then dropped him with an RKO. Thanks to Orton, Kofi lost the championship due to a disqualification.

Kofi may have been down after his fight with Orton, but he never gave up. It made him stronger—but it left him bitter. For a while, it looked like the nice-guy Superstar was gone for good.

In April 2010, Kofi was drafted to *SmackDown*. He quickly sent a message by running into the ring and kicking Chris Jericho. In his first official *SmackDown* match, he faced Jericho—and won.

Then it looked like Kofi was ready for a fresh start. He entered an Intercontinental Championship Tournament. His first opponent was Dolph Ziggler, whose sleeperhold had taken down giants like Kane and Big Show.

Kofi whirled into the ring like a tornado, clapping his hands and getting the crowd on his side. When Ziggler wrapped him in the sleeperhold, Kofi somehow got to his feet and pulled Ziggler off of him. Then he delivered his finishing move—and won the semi-final match.

Next, Kofi faced Christian on *SmackDown* to win the Intercontinental Championship. Kofi won the match—but former champion Drew McIntyre appeared with a letter from Mr. McMahon. McIntyre had been stripped of the title, but Mr. McMahon said he could have it back.

It looked like Kofi was going to have to work a little harder to earn that championship.

A week later, Kofi got another title shot at Over the Limit. He started out strong against Drew McIntyre. He traded blows with the Sinister Scotsman, fending off the Superstar's powerful punches and kicks.

Then Kofi pounded McIntyre's shoulder into the ring post and landed a Boom Drop on the slumped Superstar. McIntyre bounced back and tried to hook Kofi with a DDT, but Kofi countered with an S.O.S.: a forward flip with a leg sweep that knocked McIntyre on his back. Kofi covered him for the pinfall, becoming Intercontinental Champion—for real this time.

But Dolph Ziggler still wanted that title, and he fought fiercely to get it. He defeated Kofi in two non-title matches. Then they faced each other in an Intercontinental Championship match on *SmackDown*.

Both men fought hard. In the end, Kofi had the advantage when he knocked Ziggler down with a Trouble in Paradise. But then Ziggler's girlfriend, Vickie Guerrero, entered the ring and started yelling at the ref. Kofi turned his head to see what happened and Ziggler jumped behind him, bringing Kofi down hard on the mat. Ziggler pinned him, and Kofi lost the championship.

But Kofi wasn't about to let go that easily. On January 7, 2011, he earned a title shot on *SmackDown*. This time, Vickie stayed out of the ring.

Both Superstars used all their best moves in that match. Kofi tried a Trouble in Paradise, but Ziggler ducked it. Ziggler got a sleeperhold on Kofi, but Kofi broke away. In the end, it was a hard hit from the turnbuckle that did Ziggler in. Kofi got the three count to win back the championship.

While Kofi pumped up his fans in the ring, Ziggler attacked him from behind. Then Vickie pointed out that Ziggler was entitled to a rematch—and he wanted it now! Even though he was hurt, Kofi agreed.

Ziggler punished Kofi with punches and kicks. But Kofi found the energy for another Trouble in Paradise, and this one worked. He defeated Ziggler twice in one night—the true test of a champion.

Kofi defended the title for about four months. He lost it on *SmackDown* to Wade Barrett, the former leader of The New Nexus.

That night, members of Barrett's new group, The Corre, flanked the ring. They waited until the ref's back was turned and then distracted Kofi. This gave Barrett the chance to lift Kofi over his head and slam him to the mat. Another bad guy had taken the championship from Kofi!

At the next WrestleMania, Kofi joined some of his friends: Big Show, Kane, and Santino Marella. They battled Wade Barrett and The Corre in an eight-man tag team match. The match ended when Big Show hit Corre member Heath Slater with a knockout punch and pinned him for the win.

And the Dreadlock Dynamo kept on winning. He earned his second United States Championship at Extreme Rules in 2011. He faced Sheamus, the Irish Superstar, in a Tables Match.

The only way to win this brutal match is to put your opponent through a table. Kofi used a Boom Drop to earn his victory over the Celtic Warrior.

He's faced fierce foes and had some brutal battles, but Kofi has always managed to come out on top. It must have something to do with his positive attitude.

"Never give up on your dreams," he says. "All your life people will tell you that you can't do it. You have to be the one to show everyone that you can and you will."